Calling All Engines!

Based on *The Railway Series* by the Rev. W. Awdry

EGMONT

In the summertime, the engines were kept busy collecting lots of visitors from the Docks.

One day, The Fat Controller told the engines an Airport was being built on Sodor. "It will bring even more visitors, so the Island must be perfect!" he said.

Thomas and Percy talked about the Airport as they moved wagons. Percy couldn't wait to see the aeroplanes.

But then 'Arry and Bert arrived.
"Stinky steamies!" 'Arry said, rudely.
Thomas thought the diesels were oily and mean!

How are steam engines and diesels different?

Steam engines, like Thomas, run on coal. Diesel engines run on diesel fuel.

Steam engines make steam. Diesels don't make steam, but sometimes they make black smoke, like poor Salty!

Diesels have horns, which they honk. Steam engines have whistles, which they loudly peep!

So steamies run on coal, whistle and make steam and diesels run on diesel fuel, have horns and don't make steam. They really are very different!

Bert and 'Arry bragged to Thomas about an important job they had to do. Thomas decided to play a trick on them. He bumped their trucks, so wood fell all over the tracks.

"Oops!" said Thomas, meanly. "Now you'll be late for your important job!" And he smugly chuffed away.

Later on, when
Thomas met Percy
in the yard, they
laughed about
Thomas' trick.
They didn't notice
that Diesel was
behind them.

"You won't want to stop me from doing the important
job," Diesel said. But Thomas decided to trick him, too.

How can Thomas trick Diesel?

Diesel needs building supplies for important job. omas has trucks of wood, bananas and bricks. He'll trick Diesel by giving him the wrong one!

Which truck would be wrong for a building site? Is it the brick truck? No. You can build walls with bricks, so that could be useful.

How about the timber truck? No. You can build roofs out of wood, so that truck could also be useful.

Can you build anything with bananas? No! So Thomas will trick Diesel by giving him the banana truck!

Thomas and Percy had to fetch steel girders from the Smelter's yard. But, when they saw Diesel 10 and his powerful claw, they were scared and left without them.

That evening, Thomas was shocked to see that Tidmouth sheds had been knocked down! The diesels' special job had been to build new ones as a surprise for the steam engines.

"Silly tricks made us too late to rebuild them," said Diesel. "And we couldn't build anything with bananas!" said The Fat Controller, crossly.

The steam engines slept in other sheds that night. Thomas stayed with Emily. He felt guilty as he knew his tricks had caused all the trouble.

That night there was a fierce storm. Strong gusts of wind ripped roofs off buildings and blew over trees! The engines were very frightened.

A few hours later, some cables on the Suspension Bridge snapped. Suddenly, the heavy bridge crashed down into the valley below.

The next morning, Thomas saw the mess. "Bust my buffers!" he cried and he hurried to Tidmouth to meet the other engines.

"Unless we clear the storm damage, we can't open the Airport on time!" The Fat Controller said, sadly.
All the engines wanted to help.

Which engine should do which job?

Edward and Henry have brick and timber trucks. Harvey has a crane arm and Thomas has his carriages, Annie and Clarabel.

Trees have fallen over the tracks. **Can Harvey clear them?** Yes! He can use his strong crane arm to move the trees.

Bricks are needed at the Airport. **Can Thomas help?** No. He only has passenger carriages. **Can Henry help?** Yes. He can take his brick trucks.

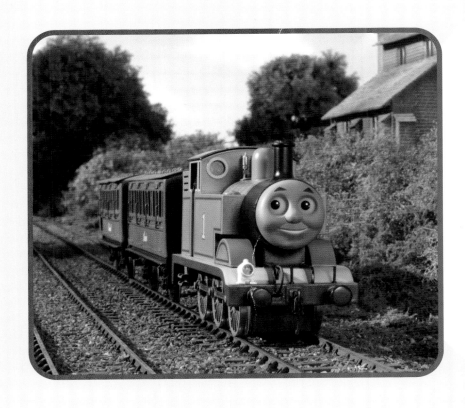

Workmen need to go and repair the Suspension Bridge. **Who can take them?** Thomas can take them, in his passenger carriages.

The Fat Controller told Thomas to take a beam to the Suspension Bridge. "It is heavy so you may need help with it," he added.

"A diesel wouldn't need any help," said Diesel, slyly. "I don't need any help either, I can do it on my own!" Thomas said, proudly.

But the beam was long and very heavy. Thomas pushed it slowly along the track.

He was going to ask 'Arry and Bert for help but they laughed at him, so he slowly went on by himself.

When Thomas got to the bridge he wanted to rest, but first he had to lift the beam into place.

Slowly, it lifted into the air. "Steam engines are better than diesels," he bragged, which made Diesel cross.

Later, when Thomas was delivering paint, he didn't see Diesel behind him. "We'll see who's best," Diesel said, as he shoved Thomas' wagon.

Splosh! Colourful paint splashed all over Thomas. Diesel laughed loudly as he rolled away.

Before long, all the diesels and steamies were fighting. They got so dirty that soon they all needed to be cleaned at the washdown.

The engines had been too busy arguing to do any of the repairs. "No visitors will want to come here!" said The Fat Controller, crossly. The engines were ashamed.

That night, the engines dreamt about what could happen if there were no visitors. Gordon dreamt he was used as a climbing frame!

Thomas dreamt about Lady and Rusty, a diesel and a steamie who worked well together. This gave him an idea, but he needed Mavis' help. He decided to find her in the morning.

How can Thomas find Mavis?

✳ Thomas knows that Mavis works at the Quarry so he will look for her there. He will also listen for her horn which goes hooonk!

⚒ At the Quarry Thomas hears a whistle. Peep! **Was it Mavis?** No, it was Percy. Mavis is a diesel so she has a horn instead of a whistle. Perhaps she is at the Docks?

Honk! **Was that Mavis' horn?** Well it was a horn, but it wasn't Mavis'. It was Salty saying "Hello" to Emily!

Maybe Mavis is having a clean at the washdown? Hooonk! **Was that Mavis' horn?** Yes, it was! Thomas has found her.

Thomas knew Mavis was a kind diesel who would help him. "Please bring the diesels to a meeting in the morning," he said. Mavis agreed. She knew something had to be done.

But Thomas was a little late for the meeting. The diesels and steam engines were about to start arguing again when he arrived.

"We have to work together," he said. "If the Airport doesn't open, we won't have any passengers or freight so we won't be Useful!"

The engines agreed that they should forget their quarrels and work together. The Fat Controller was delighted.

Which steam engine and diesel engine should work together on each job?

All the engines are good at different things. Thomas chooses which diesel engine and steam engine should work together on each job.

A small steamie is needed to help Mavis collect paint from the yard. Can Gordon help? No. He's too big. Can Percy? Yes, he's small so he can help Mavis.

Toby needs a diesel to help take workmen to the Airport. Can Bert help? No. He doesn't take passengers, but Daisy does, so she can help instead.

Gordon needs a diesel to help him take a heavy train over Gordon's Hill. Can 'Arry help? Yes! He is strong so he can help Gordon get over the hill.

With all the engines working together, the repairs were soon done. The engines were excited to hear that the first aeroplane was on its way.

But then disaster struck! As Thomas moved the last trucks, they hit a faulty buffer. They crashed across the tracks and bashed into a water tower.

The water tower fell over, making a huge crack in the runway. It had to be repaired or the aeroplane wouldn't be able to land!

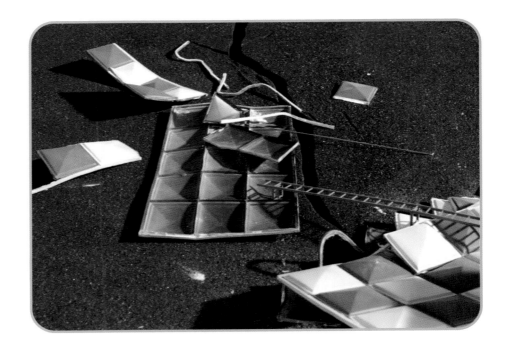

Workmen cleared the runway, but they needed George the steamroller to flatten it. And Harvey needed help clearing the fallen trucks off the tracks.

Thomas offered to fetch George and get more help. He was coupled to a flatbed truck and as soon as Harvey had cleared a track, he set off.

Thomas went to find Diesel 10. He was still a bit scared of him, but he knew Diesel 10 could help Harvey clear all the rubble off the tracks at the Airport.

Thomas timidly asked Diesel 10 for help.
"All right," Diesel 10 replied immediately. "Let's go!"
Thomas then realised that Diesel 10 wasn't scary after all!

Thomas and Diesel 10 fetched George and hurried to the Airport. The other engines were very surprised to see them together.

"Good work, George," said the workmen as he flattened the runway. It was soon ready for the aeroplane to land.

All the diesels and steam engines helped clear the tracks. "Working with diesels was fun," said Thomas. "You steamies weren't too bad either," laughed Diesel 10.

At last, the
aeroplane landed
at the Airport. The
engines all honked
their horns and
happily blew
their whistles.

That evening, the steam engines had a nice surprise.
"We have new sheds!" Thomas said, happily.

"Tidmouth sheds are bigger now, so Emily can live there, too," said The Fat Controller.
Emily was thrilled.

"I'm glad we're friends with the diesels now," said Percy. "Yes, it's good to know that like us, they just want to be Really Useful Engines!" replied Thomas, happily.

And from then on, the diesels and the steam engines were all happy to work together!

EGMONT

We bring stories to life

First published in Great Britain 2005
by Egmont Books Limited
239 Kensington High Street, London W8 6SA

Thomas the Tank Engine & Friends

A BRITT ALLCROFT COMPANY PRODUCTION

Based on The Railway Series by The Rev W Awdry

Photographs © Gullane (Thomas) Limited 2005

© Gullane (Thomas) LLC 2005

ISBN 1 4052 2164 X
1 3 5 7 9 10 8 6 4 2
Printed in Singapore